EssexWorks.

TOO
BIG!

GERALDINE McCAUGHREAN
Illustrated by Peter Bailey

For Troy

Also available in COLOUR FIRST READER books:

THE MONSTER CRISP-GUZZLER *by Malorie Blackman*
THE GHOST TEACHER *by Tony Bradman*
HAPPY MOUSEDAY *by Dick King-Smith*
INVISIBLE VINNIE *by Jenny Nimmo*
UNUSUAL DAY *by Sandi Toksvig*
THE DINOSAUR'S PACKED LUNCH *by Jacqueline Wilson*
THE MONSTER STORY-TELLER *by Jacqueline Wilson*

TOO BIG!
A CORGI BOOK 978 0 552 56581 3

Published in Great Britain by Corgi Books,
an imprint of Random House Children's Books
A Random House Group Company

Corgi Pups edition published 1999
This Colour First Reader edition published 2012

1 3 5 6 9 10 8 6 4 2

Text copyright © Geraldine McCaughrean, 1999
Illustrations copyright © Peter Bailey, 1999

The right of Geraldine McCaughrean to be identified as the author of this work
has been asserted in accordance with the Copyright, Designs and Patents Act 1988.

Set in Bembo MT Schoolbook

Corgi Books are published by Random House Children's Books,
61–63 Uxbridge Road, London W5 5SA

www.**kids**at**randomhouse**.co.uk
www.**totallyrandombooks**.co.uk
www.**randomhouse**.co.uk

Addresses for companies within The Random House Group Limited
can be found at: www.randomhouse.co.uk/offices.htm

THE RANDOM HOUSE GROUP Limited Reg. No. 954009

A CIP catalogue record for this book is available from the British Library.

Printed in China

The Random House Group Limited supports The Forest Stewardship Council (FSC®), the leading international
forest certification organisation. Our books carrying the FSC label are printed on FSC® certified paper. FSC is
the only forest certification scheme endorsed by the leading environmental organisations, including Greenpeace.
Our paper procurement policy can be found at www.randomhouse.co.uk/environment

CONTENTS

COLOUR FIRST READER books are perfect for beginner readers. All the text inside this Colour First Reader book has been checked and approved by a reading specialist, so it is the ideal size, length and level for children learning to read.

Series Reading Consultant: Prue Goodwin
Reading and Language Information Centre,
University of Reading

CHAPTER ONE
The Jumper

Dad said the tree in the back garden was too big.

"The roots will damage the house," he said. "The roots take water away from the flowers. It's too big."

But Neil liked the tree. In
the mornings its leaves cast a
quivering shadow-pattern on
his bedroom wall. What is more,
it was the ideal tree for a tree-
house. Neil had asked and asked
to have a tree-house. Mum said,
"Perhaps, when you are bigger."

But now that Dad had made up
his mind the tree was Too Big,
it looked as if the tree would be
gone before Neil had time to get
any bigger.

It was Saturday. Neil wanted to swing on the rope tied to a branch of the big old tree. It might be his last chance. But Mum wanted to take him to the shops.

"I am looking for a new wardrobe," she said, "and you need a new jumper."

"Aaah, Mu-u-um!" groaned Neil.

He did not mean to sound
ungrateful, but he and his
mother could never agree about
clothes.

Other mothers looked for the
label in the neck of a shirt, read
6–7 years, and said: "Ah! This is
perfect for my child, who is six
(or seven)."

Not Neil's mum. She looked
at the label and took out the
shirt behind – the one marked
8–9 years. "You need plenty of
room to grow!" she would say.

Unfortunately, Neil never had time to grow into a shirt before she bought him another, two sizes bigger. All Neil's clothes were too big. They made him feel like a pea in an egg-cup.

They went to
the shopping
mall and
tried on green
jumpers and

yellow jumpers,
school jumpers
and cricket
jumpers.

"I like this,"
said Neil,
pretending to
bowl a cricket
ball.

"So do I," said his mother.
He could hardly believe it!
The cricket jumper fitted him
perfectly.

"I really, really
like this," Neil said,
pretending to swing
a cricket bat.

"So do I," said
Mum. She called
the assistant.
"We will take
this one ..."

she said in her special shopping
voice. (Could this really be true?
Was she really going to buy

Neil a jumper which fitted him?)
"...if you have it in a bigger size."

Neil did complain a bit, it's
true. "Too big," he said, more
than once. "Too big, *too big*,
toobigtoobigtoobig!" But his
mum only got cross and walked
faster, so that Neil had
to run to keep
up. His sleeves
flapped
below his
fingertips,
ribbing
rippled

round his legs. Soon he had
no more breath to say, "Too
big". But he felt like a satsuma
wearing an orange peel.

Mum led the way to the
furniture store, to look at
wardrobes. She looked at pine
wardrobes and oak wardrobes,

cheap and expensive wardrobes, old, modern and Swedish wardrobes. Sometimes when she opened the door, there was a mirror inside, and Neil saw himself, huge in his jumper. He looked like a cushion in a pillowcase.

"What do you think?" said his mother.

"Too big," said Neil. Mum made a cross, gasping noise.

Some of the wardrobes had mirrors on the *outside*. Big white ghosts loomed up in the glass, and all of them were Neil in his cricket jumper.

"What do you think of this one?" said his mother.

"Too big," said Neil.

Mum was so cross that she almost stamped. "I'll take this one," she said to the shop assistant, so fiercely that he jumped backwards and fell over a bed.

"Too big!
Toobigtoobigtoobig!" said
Neil, until his mother rounded
on him with a pointing finger.

"If you don't stop complaining
about that jumper, Neil Willis,
I shall stop your pocket money!"

"But I—" The boy in the mirror waved two sorrowful, dangling sleeve-ends in protest.

He looked like a lamb in sheep's clothing.

CHAPTER TWO

The Door

The furniture store delivered the
wardrobe on Friday. It came in a
big van – too big for the garden
gate. So two men had to carry
the wardrobe all the way up the
front path.

Mum saw them coming,
opened the front door and went
out, smiling.

The men looked at the door,
they looked at the wardrobe.
"Do you have French windows,
missus?" they asked.

"No. Why?"

Well, they turned the wardrobe
on its side,

they turned
it on its end,

they opened the doors and they
took off the door-knobs.

But the wardrobe just *would not* go through the front door. It would not go through the back door either, nor the living-room window.

"I told you at the store," said Neil. "I said it was too big."

His mother glared at him in
a quite unreasonable way. And
while she glared, and talked about
cricket jumpers, the men from
the store put down the wardrobe
and crept away to their van.

"Stop! You'll have to take it
back!" called Mum. But they
had already gone.

So when Dad came home, he asked, "Why is there a wardrobe in the front garden?"

Mum explained. (She looked like Neil when he had to explain about breaking the towel rail or losing his school bag. He felt quite sorry for her.) When Dad finished being cross with Mum for buying a wardrobe too big to fit through the door, he said, "I'm sure *I* can get it indoors."

He turned it on its side, he
turned it on its end. He took off
the feet and the door-knobs.

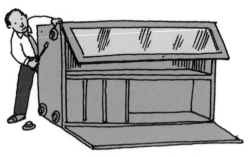

He tried it upside-down and back
to front.

But the front door refused to let
the wardrobe into the house.

"Telephone the store and tell
them to take it back," said Dad.
"It cost too much anyway."

Just as he spoke, it started
to rain. The rain drummed on
the wardrobe, trickled down
the mirror and dripped off
the hinges.

"You can't send it back now," said Neil helpfully. "It's too wet."

CHAPTER THREE

The Jitney

Dad had a stroke of genius.

"We can use the window in Neil's room! That's huge! The wardrobe will go through it easily, if we take out the whole window."

"Take out the window?" said his wife doubtfully. "You?"

"I mean I'll ask a carpenter to take out the window. Then we can just haul the wardrobe through!"

"Too big," said Neil. But his parents were busy screwing the knobs back onto the wet wardrobe, and paid no attention.

Mr Bryant down the road was a carpenter. He came along and took out the window of  Neil's room. Dad untied the rope from the branch of the big old tree and lashed it round the wardrobe. Then he fetched another from the garage, and together he and Mr Bryant stood at Neil's window and pulled.

The wardrobe rocked on its four corners. The carpenter and Dad almost pulled themselves out of the window. But apart from that, nothing happened.

"Too big," said Neil unwisely. "I told you so."

"It is not too big,"
explained his father
waspishly. "It is simply too *heavy*."

Neil's dad was not one to be defeated (especially in front of Mr Bryant).  "We shall have to hire a jitney!" he said, pointing one finger in the air.

"What's a jitney?" asked Neil.

"Yes, what is a jitney?" asked Neil's mum.

"A fork-lift truck!" said Mr Bryant delightedly. "Oh, what fun!"

"Too big," said Neil, but his parents and Mr Bryant were

busy looking in the telephone directory for companies with heavy machinery for hire.

The jitney, when it came, was not too big to fit through the gate. It was a slender, elegant machine painted bright red, with two silver prongs sticking out at the front.

The whole street turned out
to watch it trundle down the
middle of the road and swing in
at Number Fourteen. It rattled
up the path and turned left round
the side of the house. It had to
cross the vegetable patch, but that
could not be helped.

Neil, who was tired of being ignored, sat on the fence and watched. He watched the jitney uproot the carrots and harvest the cabbages. He watched it sink up to its axles, and stop.

The vegetable patch was
damp and newly dug. The jitney
got caught in it like a dinosaur
falling into a tar pit.

All the neighbours came
running to pull it out, but

the driver refused to try again.
He said the jitney would sink
into the back lawn as easily as
into the vegetable patch.

"It's too big, you mean?" said
Neil's dad through gritted teeth.

"Not too big," the driver said, patting his vehicle fondly on her shiny red bumper. "Just too heavy."

CHAPTER FOUR

Now, Everyone

"You could always use the tree," said Neil.

Dad tut-tutted. "We all know how much you like that tree," he said, "but this is no time to be discussing trees."

By now, everyone who lived in the street stood about in the garden of Number Fourteen, discussing how to get a wardrobe through an upstairs window.

"What you
need is a crane,"
said Mr Ambrose.
"Too big," said
the jitney driver.

"You could
leave it where it
is and use it for
storing your garden
tools," suggested
Mrs Blenny.

"No, no," said Mum. "It was
much too expensive for that!"

"You could make a hole in the
wall," suggested Mr Stanley, "and
carry it up the staircase."

45

 "Too big," said Neil, and Mr Stanley nodded in agreement. The wardrobe would never fit between the banisters.

"Why don't you throw a rope over the top branch of that tree and use it like a pulley?" said Mrs Hogg.

"What a good idea, Mrs Hogg," said Dad.

Neil sank his head into his hands and sighed. Why did no-one ever listen to him?

This was the plan:

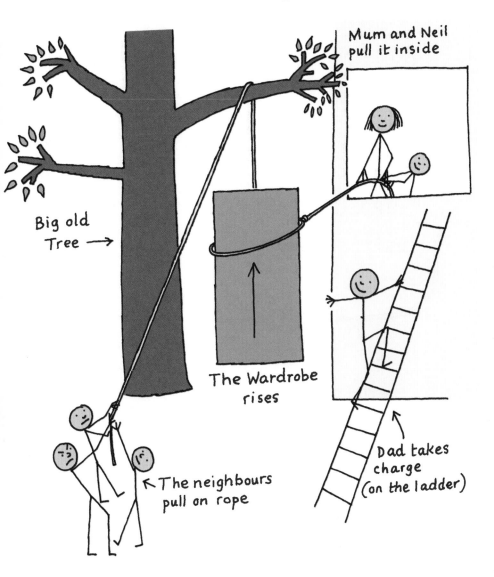

Easy.

Dad stood on the ladder. Mum and Neil stood in the bedroom window (because Dad said that was the easy part). The neighbours all took hold of the rope, then Dad counted down from ten backwards and they *pulled*.

The wardrobe started to lift, like a rocket taking off for the moon. Up and up it went. The sun flashed in its mirrored doors. It was easy.

"This jumper is too big,"
Neil told his mother, as the
wardrobe rose into sight outside.

"Not now, Neil," Mum said,
pulling on the rope to swing the
wardrobe in over the sill. "The
curtains are catching. Just hold
the rope while I free them . . ."

Neil tried. He really did. He made a grab for the rope, but the sleeves of his new cricket jumper were dangling down over his fingers, and he just could not get a grip.

The rope slipped through his droopy woollen cuffs, and the wardrobe swung out and away from the house, like Tarzan on a jungle creeper.

It knocked over the ladder
with Dad on it, and crashed up
against the tree, wedging itself
between two branches.

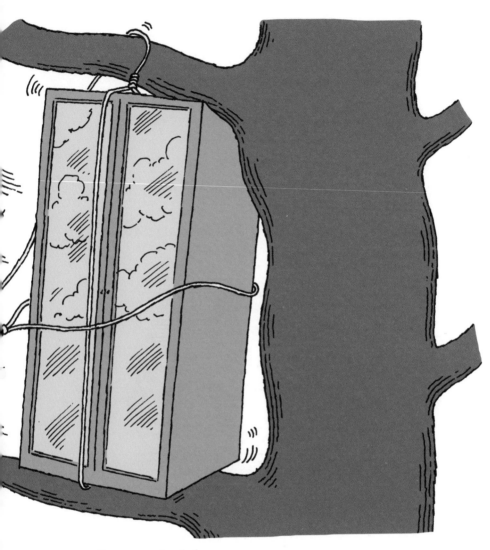

The neighbours were
so scared by the loud noise that
they let go of their rope.

Neil poked his head out of the window and flapped his sleeve-ends.

"Sorry!" he called. "My jumper was too big, you see!"

CHAPTER FIVE

Just Right

Mrs Blenny looked up at the wardrobe in the tree. "Just right," she said.

Mr Stanley agreed. "Just right."

"I always wanted one when I was a lad," said the jitney-driver.

"Couldn't have built a finer one myself," said Mr Bryant.

"But Mum wanted a new wardrobe, and Dad wants to cut down the tree," said Neil.

There was an angry murmur among the neighbours.

"Cut down the tree?" said Mr Ambrose. "But we can see that tree from all over. It's a fine old tree!"

"A person can't just *cut down* a tree!" said Mrs Hogg hotly. "There are laws!"

"No, no. Of course not," said Dad, turning an odd shade of pink.

"It's a local landmark,"
Mr Ambrose insisted.

"Yes, yes. Of course
it is," said Dad.

"Especially with a tree-house
in it," said the jitney-driver.

It was true: the wardrobe made a
wonderful tree-house. The ladder
just reached to it. The inside was
big enough for a boy, while the
shelves on one side held plenty of

books and toys, and secret things
like telescopes and signal flags
and pieces of rope.

That summer holiday, Neil
spent all his time going up and
down the ladder. The weather
was warm. He wore T-shirts
and shorts. They were still one
or two sizes too big, but Neil
did not care.

His tree-house was just the
right size.

THE END!

THE **GHOST TEACHER**

TONY BRADMAN

ILLUSTRATED BY
PETER KAVANAGH

Also
available as

★ ★ ★ COLOUR FIRST READER ★ ★ ★

The **MONSTER** CRISP-GUZZLER

MALORIE BLACKMAN

Illustrated by
SAMI SWEETEN

★ COLOUR ★
FIRST
READERS

★ ★ ★ COLOUR FIRST READER ★ ★ ★

HAPPY MOUSE DAY

DICK KING-SMITH

Illustrated by
PETER KAVANAGH

★ ★ ★ COLOUR FIRST READER ★ ★ ★

UNUSUAL ★ DAY ★

SANDI TOKSVIG
Illustrated by GEORGIEN OVERWATER

★ ★ ★ COLOUR FIRST READER ★ ★ ★

INVISIBLE VINNIE

JENNY NIMMO
Illustrated by SUE HEAP

★ ★ ★ COLOUR FIRST READER ★ ★ ★

Jacqueline Wilson

The Dinosaur's Packed Lunch

Illustrated by
Nick Sharratt

★ ★ ★ COLOUR FIRST READER ★ ★ ★

Jacqueline Wilson

The Monster Story-Teller

Illustrated by
Nick Sharratt